The Railway Series No. 29

GREAT LITTLE ENGINES

CHRISTOPHER AWDRY

with illustrations by
CLIVE SPONG

HEINEMANN · LONDON

The author would like to thank fellow-members of the Talyllyn Railway
Preservation Society for help in the preparation of this book.

First published in Great Britain 1985
Reprinted 1993 by William Heinemann Ltd
an imprint of Reed Children's Books
Michelin House, 81 Fulham Rd, London SW3 6RB
and Auckland, Melbourne, Singapore and Toronto

ISBN 0 434 92806 2

Printed and bound in Great Britain by
William Clowes Limited, Beccles and London

DEAR FRIENDS,

Sir Handel has been helping on the Talyllyn Railway, at Tywyn, in Wales.

"You could write a book about it," he said when I went to see him.

Sir Handel was conceited before he went: whatever would happen, I thought, if he had a book all to himself? But some of his adventures *were* too good to waste, so I mixed them with stories about the other engines. That ought to keep everyone happy.

THE AUTHOR

Patience is a Virtue

THE Thin Controller held a letter in his hand. Six little engines watched him anxiously.

"Do you remember Talyllyn, your 'Twin'?" he asked Skarloey. "He is ill, so his Controller is short of an engine. Now, I can't spare anyone until Duke is mended, but I want to suggest to him that one of us . . ."

"Oh, Sir, please, Sir!" cried the engines excitedly.

The Thin Controller held his ears.

"You can't all go," he laughed. "I thought . . . Sir Handel."

"Oh, Sir," said Sir Handel happily.

A few days later Duke was taken to the Works. Sir Handel's excitement grew.

"I hope he comes back quickly," he said to anyone who would listen.

"Don't be so impatient," his driver laughed. "There's a lot to be done. Your repairs took a long time, remember, and Duke is older than you."

The weeks passed, and still Duke didn't come back. Sir Handel became more and more impatient. One day he was waiting at the bottom station when Gordon arrived.

"I've been invited to Wales," Sir Handel told him importantly, "but I can't be spared until Duke is mended."

"Quite right," said Gordon. "It's a great responsibility being indispensible."

"Gordon says I'm ... er ... insensible," Sir Handel boasted to the others.

They were amused, but not impressed.

Summer came, and crowds of visitors came to the railway. Sometimes extra coaches were needed to carry them all. One day Sir Handel's train was fuller than ever. When he reached the top station he was exhausted.

An enormous crowd of people was waiting on the platform for the last train home.

"They must have come on earlier trains and stayed to picnic by the lake," said the fireman. "Never mind, we'll manage. It's all downhill now."

But at the station near the waterfall the platform was full too.

"We need a shoehorn to get them all in!" exclaimed the guard, scratching his head. "Still, we'll have to do it somehow. I'll take some with me in Beatrice."

The passengers had enjoyed their day in the hills, and didn't mind standing. They knew it would be for only a short while.

The Guard always checked tickets at the station by the waterfall. Today it was a long job, and before he had half finished Sir Handel was growing impatient.

"An insensible engine like me shouldn't keep Henry waiting," he fumed.

"Can't be helped," said his driver. "Henry will just have to wait – he's kept us at it before now."

At last the Guard was ready. He blew his whistle, waved his green flag and turned towards Beatrice.

"At last we're off, do come along, at last we're off, do come along," Sir Handel snorted impatiently. Quickly the train began to move.

The Guard tried to get into Beatrice, but her doorway was blocked by passengers. By the time they had moved to let him in, the train was out of the station and the Guard was left standing on the platform.

Beatrice tried to stop, but there was no one to put her brakes on. The Guard blew his whistle and waved a red flag, but the line curved, and Sir Handel couldn't see or hear him. Luckily a passenger in Beatrice knew what to do. He pressed a button, and a buzzer sounded in Sir Handel's cab. His driver braked, hard.

"Now what?" he asked the fireman. "Go and find out – maybe we've left someone behind."

They had, of course. They soon discovered who.

Passengers helped the Guard into Beatrice, and after a fast run the train reached the terminus at the same time as Henry. Sir Handel stopped with a sigh of relief.

The Guard came to see him.

"I'm sorry I was impatient Mr Guard," said Sir Handel nervously. "I didn't want to be late – insensible engines shouldn't be late, should they?"

"No," agreed the Guard. "But *sensible* engines know that patience *is* a virtue. Remember that next time."

"I'll try," promised Sir Handel sadly.

Peter Sam and the Prickly Problem

DUKE returned at last, and Sir Handel went away. The other engines were kept so busy that they didn't have time to miss him.

Hedgecutters had been busy too, trimming trees and bushes beside the railway so that passengers could see the view.

Each evening Rusty took some trucks up the line and carried away as many cuttings as he could. But he could manage only a few at a time, and as fast as he moved the cuttings, more took their place.

It was Peter Sam's turn to take the morning train. The coaches were full, but the rails were dry and Peter Sam didn't mind the extra load. He puffed happily along until, just beyond the tunnel, he found that, in the night, a high wind had blown hedge-cuttings across the rails.

He stopped, and his driver and fireman got down.

"We'll never get through that lot!" exclaimed the fireman.

"Pooh!" scoffed Peter Sam. "They're only little branches. Nothing to it – we'll simply push them aside."

"Have it your own way," said his driver. "If we stop to clear up properly we shall be here for ages and some of the passengers might miss their train at the bottom station."

Peter Sam puffed bravely on. He went carefully at first, and the branches slid aside easily. Then came a stretch where the cuttings were brambles. Peter Sam began to regret his boasting. Not only were the thorns prickly, but they caught in each other, and the branches stayed firmly put.

"Ouch!" exclaimed Peter Sam suddenly, and stopped. "I can't move," he complained.

The fireman looked.

"It's no good," he said at last. "You've got brambles caught in your valve gear, and steam can't get into your cylinders. We shall have to cut you out."

Peter Sam shuddered. He shut his eyes and prepared for the worst.

The fireman pulled on thick gloves. Then, while he tried to clear what he could, the driver went to ask the Guard if he had a knife.

Some of the passengers had knives too, and came to help. But even then the job took longer than expected, and by the time Peter Sam was free there was no hope of getting the passengers round the lake and back before James's train left.

Peter Sam's driver apologised to the passengers, but they said they didn't mind.

"We enjoyed the adventure," they laughed.

The driver telephoned the Thin Controller. On the way home they passed Rusty, pulling a long train of trucks.

Rusty worked hard, and by afternoon the line was clear for trains to run normally.

Peter Sam's front felt uncomfortable for several days. The others laughed, and teased him.

"Take a snowplough next time," they suggested, and they kept asking if he had a sharp knife in his cab.

At last Skarloey told them to stop.

"I really can't think what all the fuss is for," remarked Duncan innocently. "They were only little branches, after all – nothing to get prickly about, surely."

"Pop" Special

DURING the summer a party of Scouts set up tents in a field beside the line. They bustled about arranging things, but were never too busy to wave to the engines as they passed.

"They've come for their annual 'Camp'," explained Duncan's driver. "It's a sort of holiday for them. Their Leader has been to see Mr Hugh, and he says that the boys can work on the railway for us."

"Sounds a funny sort of holiday to me," said Duncan doubtfully.

"Lots of people do it," continued the driver. "The Talyllyn Railway, where Sir Handel has gone, has most of its work done like that. The Scouts are going to help us. You know that place near the top station, where the ditches are bad and we have to be careful when it's wet? Well, the Scouts are going to put that right for us."

The engines were pleased, because they didn't like having to slow down there in wet or frosty weather.

It was anything but frosty at present. Each day the sun shone, and it became hotter and hotter, too hot even for holidaymakers to lie on the beach. Every train was full.

The Scouts were hot too. They rested thankfully as the trains passed, but their cheerful waves became wearier as the week wore on.

On the final day of their "Camp," Duncan toiled uphill with the last train. He was looking forward to a rest under the trees at the top station.

As Duncan neared the place where the Scouts were working, he whistled to warn them he was coming.

Then he saw a figure crossing the line in front of the train. Duncan's driver put a hand on his brake.

"Steady on Duncan," he warned. "It looks as if the Scouts' Leader wants us to stop for something."

Duncan drew gently to a halt, and the Leader climbed onto the step of his cab.

"Is anything wrong?" the driver asked anxiously.

"Not yet," replied the Leader, "but I'm afraid there might be unless the boys have a drink. Can you drop off some 'pop' or something when you next pass, please?"

"No problem," replied the driver. "I'll see the refreshment lady when we reach the top station."

But when they got there, the driver came back from the refreshment room with a long face.

"Not a bottle to be had," he moaned to Duncan. "Everyone's as thirsty as those boys. So now what?"

Duncan didn't know. He thought so hard that he began to feel thirsty himself. Then, suddenly, an idea came to him. "Isn't there a shop near the station by the lake?" he said. "Perhaps the lady there . . ."

"Of course!" interrupted the fireman excitedly. "We'll leave the coaches here while Duncan takes something to the boys. We can just get back here before the train is due to leave, but we must hurry."

While the Stationmaster telephoned to warn the shop-lady, Duncan set off.

The shop-lady met them at the station.

"I haven't much myself," she said, "but the lads are welcome to what there is."

A little later the Scouts heard a whistle and Duncan puffed into sight. He stopped beside them, and his driver handed down the drinks.

The Scouts cheered him.

"Not me," he told them. "It was Duncan's idea."

So they cheered again, and thanked Duncan instead.

"It's nothing," he said modestly, "you're helping us – its only fair we should help you too."

Sir Handel Comes Home

SIR HANDEL was given a great welcome when he returned. It was too late for the workmen to unload him that night, so the engines asked if his truck could be put where he could tell them about his adventures.

"A real Prince and Princess came to see us," Sir Handel told them proudly. "They rode in a special train. Driver said they were given some books about us written by someone called the Thin Clergyman, but I didn't really understand that."

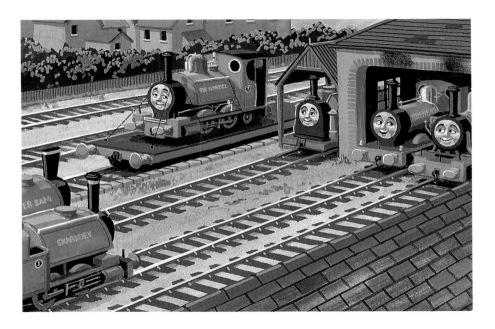

"I do," said Duke. "He and the Fat Clergyman were the ones who found me, and they put me in a book too."

Peter Sam was impressed.

"Did you pull the Prince's train?" he asked Sir Handel.

"No," replied Sir Handel. "I was spare engine – it poured with rain and I got soaked. I pulled a special wedding train though. We had to bring the coaches back very early in the morning. I've never been out at that time of day before."

Peter Sam told Sir Handel about his tangle with the brambles. Sir Handel laughed.

"I know what you mean," he said. "I had an adventure a bit like that just before I came away. It was a wet day, and I didn't want to go out, but driver said I must. Well, we set off. Luckily the train wasn't very full, so we got on all right, even though it was raining. Then we stopped at a station . . ."

Sir Handel paused dramatically.

"Go on," urged Peter Sam.

"Just beyond the station," continued Sir Handel, "there was a steep bit and a curve. Well, it was wet, so naturally I was concentrating on getting up the hill."

"Of course," agreed Rheneas gravely.

"As we came round the bend a tree suddenly seemed to jump out at me. I tried to stop, of course, but my wheels slipped on the wet rails, and I ran smack into the tree. It hurt, I can tell you."

"It must have done," agreed Duke, and there were sympathetic murmurs from the others.

"The tree didn't actually hit me in the eye," explained Sir Handel, "but driver and fireman made a great fuss about it. Next morning they put a bandage on my forehead and a black patch over one eye. Everyone laughed, and said I looked like a pirate. Then I pulled a special train at something they called an AGM. They even wrote a piece about me in their magazine."

Sir Handel sighed happily.

"Oh, it was great fun," he said.

"Did you see my 'Twin', Talyllyn?" asked Skarloey.

"He was in another part of the Shed," replied Sir Handel. "The other engines told me that he's on the mend and he'll be back at work soon. He's lucky – he's got a lovely railway."

Sir Handel closed his eyes, remembering.

"All the same," he added, "it's good to be home."

Duke smiled in the darkness.

"I know what you mean," he agreed.